Brother Jacob

George Eliot

A Phoenix Paperback

This edition published in 1996 by Phoenix
a division of Orion Books Ltd
Orion House, 5 Upper St Martin's Lane, London WC2H 9EA

ISBN 1 85799 744 1

Typeset by Deltatype Ltd, Ellesmere Port, Cheshire
Printed in Great Britain by Clays Ltd, St Ives plc

BROTHER JACOB

Trompeurs, c'est pour vous que j'écris,
Attendez vous à la pareille

LA FONTAINE

CHAPTER I

Among the many fatalities attending the bloom of young desire, that of blindly taking to the confectionery line has not, perhaps, been sufficiently considered. How is the son of a British yeoman, who has been fed principally on salt pork and yeast dumplings, to know that there is satiety for the human stomach even in a paradise of glass jars full of sugared almonds and pink lozenges, and that the tedium of life can reach a pitch where plum-buns at discretion cease to offer the slightest enticement? Or how, at the tender age when a confectioner seems to him a very prince whom all the world must envy, – who breakfasts on macaroons, dines on marengs, sups on twelfth-cake, and fills up the intermediate hours with sugar-candy or peppermint, – how is he to foresee the day of sad wisdom, when he will discern that the confectioner's calling is not socially influential, or favourable to a soaring ambition? I have known a man who turned out to have a metaphysical genius, incautiously, in the period of youthful buoyancy, commence his career as a dancing-master; and you may imagine the use that was made of this initial mistake by opponents who felt themselves bound to warn the public against his doctrine of the Inconceivable. He could not give up his dancing-lessons, because he made his bread by them, and metaphysics would not have found him in so much as salt to his bread. It was really the same with Mr David Faux and the confectionery business. His uncle, the butler at the great house close by Brigford, had made a pet of him in his early boyhood, and it was on a visit to this uncle that the confectioners' shops in that brilliant town had, on a single day, fired his tender imagination. He carried home the pleasing illusion that a confectioner must be at once the happiest and the foremost of men since the things he made were not only the most beautiful to behold, but the very best eating, and such as the Lord Mayor must always order largely for his private recreation; so that when his father declared he must be put to a trade, David chose his line without a moment's hesitation; and, with a rashness inspired by a sweet tooth, wedded himself irrevocably to confectionery. Soon, however, the tooth lost its relish and fell into bland indifference; and all the while, his mind expanded, his ambition took new shapes, which could hardly be satisfied within the sphere his youthful ardour had chosen. But what was he to do? He was a young man of much mental activity, and, above all, gifted with a spirit of contrivance; but then, his faculties would not tell with great effect in any other medium than that of candied sugars, conserves, and pastry. Say what you will about the identity of the reasoning process in all branches of thought, or about the advantage of coming to subjects with a fresh mind the adjustment of butter to flour, and of heat to pastry, is *not* the best preparation for the office of prime minister; besides, in the present imperfectly-organised state of society, there are social barriers. David could invent delightful things in the way of drop-cakes, and he had the widest views of the sugar department; but in other directions he certainly felt hampered by the want of knowledge and practical skill; and the world is so inconveniently constituted, that the vague consciousness of being a fine fellow is no guarantee of success in any line of business.

This difficulty pressed with some severity on Mr David Faux, even before his apprenticeship was ended. His soul swelled with an impatient sense that he ought to become something very remarkable – that it was quite out of the question for him to put up with a narrow lot as other men did: he scorned the idea that he could accept an average. He was sure there was nothing average about him: even such a person as Mrs Tibbits, the washer-woman, perceived it, and probably had a preference for his linen. At that particular period he was weighing out gingerbread-nuts; but such an anomaly could not continue. No position could be suited to Mr David Faux that was not in the highest degree easy to the flesh and flattering to the spirit. If he had fallen on the present times, and enjoyed the advantages of a Mechanics' Institute, he would certainly have taken to literature. He had read some novels from the adjoining circulating library, and had even bought the story of 'Inkle and Yarico', which had made him feel very sorry for poor Mr Inkle; so that his ideas might not have been below a certain mark of the literary calling; but his spelling and diction were too unconventional.

When a man is not adequately appreciated or comfortably placed in his own country, his thoughts naturally turn towards foreign climes; and David's imagination circled round and round the utmost limits of his geographical knowledge, in search of a country where a young gentleman of pasty visage, lipless mouth, and stumpy hair, would be likely to be received with the hospitable enthusiasm which he had a right to expect. Having a general idea of America as a country where the population was chiefly black, it appeared to him the most propitious destination for an emigrant who, to begin with, had the most broad and easily recognisable merit of whiteness; and this idea gradually took such strong possession of him that he might emigrate under easier circumstances, if he supplied himself with a little money from his master's till. But that evil spirit, whose understanding, I am convinced, has been much overrated, quite wasted his time on this occasion. David would certainly have liked well to have some of his master's money in his pocket, if he had been sure his master would have been the only man to suffer for it; but he was a cautious youth, and quite determined to run no risks on his own account. So he stayed out his apprenticeship, and committed no act of dishonesty that was at all likely to be discovered, reserving his plan of emigration for a future opportunity. And the circumstances under which he carried it out were in this wise. Having been at home a week or two partaking of the family beans, he had used his leisure in ascertaining a fact which was of considerable importance to him, namely, that his mother had a small sum in guineas painfully saved from her maiden perquisites, and kept in the corner of a drawer where her baby-linen had reposed for the last twenty years – ever since her son David had taken to

his feet, with a slight promise of bow-legs which had not

been altogether unfulfilled. Mr Faux, senior, had told his son very frankly, that he must not look to being set-up in business by *him*; with seven sons, and one of them a very healthy and well-developed idiot, who consumed a dumpling about eight inches in diameter every day, it was pretty well if they got a hundred apiece at his death. Under these circumstances, what was David to do? It was certainly hard that he should take his mother's money; but he saw no other ready means of getting any, and it was not to be expected that a young man of his merit should put up with inconveniences that could be avoided. Besides, it is not robbery to take property belonging to your mother: she doesn't prosecute you. And David was very well behaved to his mother; he comforted her by speaking highly of himself to her, and assuring her that he never fell into the vices he saw practised by other youths of his own age, and that he was particularly fond of honesty. If his mother would have given him her twenty guineas as a reward of this noble disposition, he really would not have stolen them from her, and it would have been more agreeable to his feelings. Nevertheless, to an active mind like David's, ingenuity is not without its pleasures: it was rather an interesting occupation to become stealthily acquainted with the wards of his mother's simple key (not in the least like Chubb's patent), and to get one that would do its work equally well; and also to arrange a little drama by which he would escape suspicion, and run no risk of forfeiting the prospective hundred at his father's death, which would be convenient in the improbable case of his *not* making a large fortune in the 'Indies'.

First, he spoke freely of his intention to start shortly for Liverpool and take ship for America; a resolution which cost his good mother some pain, for, after Jacob the idiot, there was not one of her sons to whom her heart clung more than to her youngest-born, David. Next, it appeared to him that Sunday afternoon, when everybody was gone to church except Jacob and the cow-boy, was so singularly favourable an opportunity for sons who wanted to appropriate their mothers' guineas, that he half thought it must have been kindly intended by Providence for such purposes. Especially the third Sunday in Lent; because Jacob had been out on one of his occasional wanderings for the last two days; and David, being a timid young man, had a considerable dread and hatred of Jacob, as of a large personage who went about habitually with a pitchfork in his hand.

Nothing could be easier, then, than for David on this Sunday afternoon to decline going to church, on the ground that he was going to tea at Mr Lunn's, whose pretty daughter Sally had been an early flame of his, and, when the church-goers were at a safe distance, to abstract the guineas from their wooden box and slip them into a small canvas bag – nothing easier than to call to the cow-boy that he was going, and tell him to keep an eye on the house for fear of Sunday tramps. David thought it would be easy, too, to get to a small thicket and bury his bag in a hole he had already made and covered up under the roots of an old hollow ash, and he had, in fact, found the hole without a moment's difficulty, had uncovered it, and was about gently to drop the bag into it, when the sound of a large body rustling towards him with something like a bellow was such a surprise to David, who, as a gentleman gifted with much contrivance, was naturally only prepared for what he expected, that instead of dropping the bag gently he let it fall so as to make it untwist and vomit forth the shining guineas. In the same moment he looked up and saw his dear brother Jacob close upon him, holding the pitchfork so that the bright smooth prongs were a yard in advance of his own body, and about a foot off David's. (A learned friend, to whom I once narrated this history, observed that it was David's guilt which made these prongs formidable, and that the *mens nil conscia sibi* strips a pitchfork of all terrors. I thought this idea so valuable, that I obtained his leave to use it on condition of suppressing his name.) Nevertheless, David did not entirely lose his presence of mind; for in that case he would have sunk on the earth or started backward; whereas he kept his ground and smiled at Jacob, who nodded his head up and down, and said, 'Hoich, Zavy!' in a painfully equivocal manner. David's heart was beating audibly, and if he had had any lips they would have been pale; but his mental activity, instead of being paralysed, was stimulated. While he was inwardly praying (he always prayed when he was much frightened), – 'Oh, save me this once, and I'll never get into danger again!' – he was thrusting his hand into his pocket in search of a box of yellow lozenges, which he had brought with him from Brigford among other delicacies of the same portable kind, as a means of conciliating proud beauty, and more particularly the beauty of Miss Sarah Lunn. Not one of these delicacies had he ever offered to poor Jacob, for David was not a young man to waste his jujubes and barley-sugar in giving pleasure to people from whom he expected nothing. But an idiot with equivocal intentions and a pitchfork is as well worth flattering and cajoling as if he were Louis Napoleon. So David, with a promptitude equal to the occasion, drew out his box of yellow lozenges, lifted the lid, and performed a pantomine with his mouth and fingers, which was meant to imply that he was delighted to see his dear brother Jacob, and seized the opportunity of making him a small present, which he would find particularly agreeable to the taste. Jacob, you understand, was not an intense idiot, but within a certain limited range knew how to choose the good and reject the evil: he took one lozenge, by way of test, and sucked it as if he had been a philosopher; then, in as great an ecstasy at its new and complex savour as Caliban at the taste of Trinculo's wine, chuckled and stroked this suddenly beneficient brother, and held out his hand for more; for, except in fits of anger, Jacob was not ferocious or needlessly predatory. David's courage half returned, and he left off praying; pouring a dozen lozenges into Jacob's palm, and trying to look very fond of him. He congratulated himself that he had formed the plan of going to see Miss Sally Lunn this afternoon, and that, as a consequence, he had brought with him these propitiatory delicacies: he was certainly a lucky fellow; indeed, it was always likely Providence should be fonder of him than of other apprentices, and since he *was* to be interrupted, why, an idiot was preferable to any other sort of witness. For the first time in his life, David thought he saw the advantage of idiots.

10   As for Jacob, he had thrust his pitchfork into the ground,

and had thrown himself down beside it, in thorough abandonment to the unprecedented pleasure of having five lozenges in his mouth at once, blinking meanwhile, and making inarticulate sounds of gustative content. He had not yet given any sign of noticing the guineas, but in seating himself he had laid his broad right hand on them, and unconsciously kept it in that position, absorbed in the sensations of his palate. If he could only be kept so occupied with the lozenges as not to see the guineas before David could manage to cover them! That was David's best hope of safety; for Jacob knew his mother's guineas; it had been part of their common experience as boys to be allowed to look at these handsome coins, and rattle them in their box on high days and holidays, and among all Jacob's narrow experiences as to money, this was likely to be the most memorable.

'Here, Jacob,' said David, in an insinuating tone, handing the box to him, 'I'll give 'em all to you. Run! – make haste! – else somebody 'll come and take 'em.'

David, not having studied the psychology of idiots, was not aware that they are not to be wrought upon by imaginative fears. Jacob took the box with his left hand, but saw no necessity for running away. Was ever a promising young man wishing to lay the foundation of his fortune by appropriating his mother's guineas obstructed by such a day-mare as this? But the moment must come when Jacob would move his right hand to draw off the lid of the tin box, and then David would sweep the guineas into the hole with the utmost address and swiftness, and immediately seat himself upon them. Ah, no! It's of no use to have foresight when you are dealing with an idiot: he is not to be calculated upon. Jacob's right hand was given to vague clutching and throwing; it suddenly clutched the guineas as if they had been so many pebbles, and was raised in an attitude which promised to scatter them like seed over a distant bramble, when, from some prompting or other – probably of an unwonted sensation – it paused, descended to Jacob's knee, and opened slowly under the inspection of Jacob's dull eyes. David began to pray again, but immediately desisted – another resource having occurred to him.

'Mother! zinnies!' exclaimed the innocent Jacob. Then, looking at David, he said, interrogatively, 'Box?'

'Hush! hush!' said David, summoning all his ingenuity in this severe strait. 'See, Jacob!' He took the tin box from his brother's hand, and emptied it of the lozenges, returning half of them to Jacob, but secretly keeping the rest in his own hand. Then he held out the empty box, and said, 'Here's the box, Jacob! The box for the guineas!' gently sweeping them from Jacob's palm into the box.

This procedure was not objectionable to Jacob; on the contrary, the guineas clinked so pleasantly as they fell, that he wished for a reptition of the sound, and seizing the box, began to rattle it very gleefully. David, seizing the opportunity, deposited his reserve of lozenges in the ground and hastily swept some earth over them. 'Look, Jacob!' he said, at last. Jacob paused from his clinking, and looked into the hole, while David began to scratch away the earth, as if in doubtful expectation. When the lozenges were laid bare, he took them out one by one, and gave them to Jacob.

'Hush!' he said, in a loud whisper, 'Tell nobody – all for

Jacob – hush – sh – sh! Put guineas in the hole – they'll come out like this!' To make the lesson more complete, he took a guinea, and lowering it into the hole, said, 'Put in *so*.' Then, as he took the last lozenge out, he said, 'Come out *so*,' and put the lozenge into Jacob's hospitable mouth.

Jacob turned his head on one side, looked first at his brother and then at the hole, like a reflective monkey, and, finally, laid the box of guineas in the hole with much decision. David made haste to add every one of the stray coins, put on the lid, and covered it well with earth, saying in his most coaxing tone –

'Take 'm out tomorrow, Jacob; all for Jacob! Hush – sh – sh!'

Jacob, to whom this once indifferent brother had all at once become a sort of sweet-tasted fetish, stroked David's best coat with his adhesive fingers, and then hugged him with an accompaniment of that mingled chuckling and gurgling by which he was accustomed to express the milder passions. But if he had chosen to bite a small morsel out of his beneficent brother's cheek, David would have been obliged to bear it.

And here I must pause, to point out to you the short-sightedness of human contrivance. This ingenious young man, Mr David Faux, thought he had achieved a triumph of cunning when he had associated himself in his brother's rudimentary mind with the flavour of yellow lozenges. But he had yet to learn that it is a dreadful thing to make an idiot fond of you, when you yourself are not of an affectionate disposition: especially an idiot with a pitchfork – obviously a difficult friend to shake off by rough usage.

It may seem to you rather a blundering contrivance for a clever young man to bury the guineas. But, if everything had turned out as David had calculated, you would have seen that his plan was worthy of his talents. The guineas would have lain safely in the earth while the theft was discovered, and David, with the calm of conscious innocence, would have lingered at home, reluctant to say good-bye to his dear mother while she was in grief about her guineas; till at length, on the eve of his departure, he would have disinterred them in the strictest privacy, and carried them on his own person without inconvenience. But David, you perceive, had reckoned without his host, or, to speak more precisely, without his idiot brother – an item of so uncertain and fluctuating a character, that I doubt whether he would not have puzzled the astute heroes of M. de Balzac, whose foresight is so remarkably at home in the future.

It was clear to David now that he had only one alternative before him: he must either renounce the guineas, by quietly putting them back in his mother's drawer (a course not unattended with difficulty); or he must leave more than a suspicion behind him, by departing early the next morning without giving notice, and with the guineas in his pocket. For if he gave notice that he was going, his mother, he knew, would insist on fetching from her box of guineas the three she had always promised him as his share; indeed, in his original plan, he had counted on this as a means by which the theft would be discovered under circumstances that would themselves speak for his innocence; but now, as I need hardly explain, that well-combined plan was completely frustrated. Even if David could have bribed Jacob with perpetual lozenges, an idiot's secrecy is itself betrayal. He dared not even go to tea at Mr Lunns', for in that case he would have lost sight of Jacob, who, in his impatience for the crop of lozenges, might scratch up the box again while he was absent, and carry it home – depriving him at once of reputation and guineas. No! he must think of nothing all the rest of this day, but of coaxing Jacob and keeping him out of mischief. It was a fatiguing and anxious evening to David; nevertheless, he dared not go to sleep without tying a piece of string to his thumb and great toe, to secure his frequent waking; for he meant to be up with the first peep of dawn, and be far out of reach before breakfast-time. His father, he thought, would certainly cut him off with a shilling; but what then? Such a striving young man as he would be sure to be well received in the West Indies: in foreign countries there are always openings – even for cats. It was probably that some Princess Yarico would want him to marry her, and make him presents of very large jewels beforehand; after which, he needn't marry her unless he liked. David had made up his mind not to steal any more, even from people who were fond of him: it was an unpleasant way of making your fortune in a world where you were likely to be surprised in the act by brothers. Such alarms did not agree with David's constitution, and he had felt so much nausea this evening that no doubt his liver was affected. Besides, he would have been greatly hurt not to be thought well of in the world: he always meant to make a figure, and be thought worthy of the best seats and the best morsels.

Ruminating to this effect on the brilliant future in reserve for him, David by the help of his check-string kept himself on the alert to seize the time of earliest dawn for his rising and departure. His brothers, of course, were early risers, but he should anticipate them by at least an hour and a half, and the little room which he had to himself as only an occasional visitor, had its window over the horse-block, so that he could slip out through the window without the least difficulty. Jacob, the horrible Jacob, had an awkward trick of getting up before everybody else, to stem his hunger by emptying the milk-bowl that was 'duly set' for him; but of late he had taken to sleeping in the hay-loft, and if he came into the house, it would be on the opposite side to that from which David was making his exit. There was no need to think of Jacob; yet David was liberal enough to bestow a curse on him – it was the only thing he ever did bestow gratuitously. His small bundle of clothes was ready packed, and he was soon treading lightly on the steps of the horse-block, soon walking at a smart pace across the fields towards the thicket. It would take him no more than two minutes to get out the box; he could make out the tree it was under by the pale strip where the bark was off, although the dawning light was rather dimmer in the thicket. But what, in the name of – burnt pastry – was that large body with a staff planted beside it, close at the foot of the ash-tree? David paused, not to make up his mind as to the nature of the apparition – he had not the happiness of doubting for a moment that the staff was Jacob's pitchfork – but to gather the self-command necessary for addressing his brother with a sufficiently honeyed accent. Jacob was absorbed in scratching up the earth, and had not heard David's

approach.

'I say, Jacob,' said David in a loud whisper, just as the tin box was lifted out of the hole.

Jacob looked up, and discerning his sweet-flavoured brother, nodded and grinned in the dim light in a way that made him seem to David like a triumphant demon. If he had been of an impetuous disposition, he would have snatched the pitchfork from the ground and impaled this fraternal demon. But David was by no means impetuous; he was a young man greatly given to calculate consequences, a habit which has been held to be the foundation of virtue. But somehow it had not precisely that effect in David: he calculated whether an action would harm himself, or whether it would only harm other people. In the former case he was very timid about satisfying his immediate desires, but in the latter he would risk the result with much courage.

'Give it *me*, Jacob,' he said, stooping down and patting his brother. 'Let us see.'

Jacob, finding the lid rather tight, gave the box to his brother in perfect faith. David raised the lid, and shook his head, while Jacob put his finger in and took out a guinea to taste whether the metamorphosis into lozenges was complete and satisfactory.

'No, Jacob; too soon, too soon,' said David, when the guinea had been tasted. 'Give it me; we'll go and bury it somewhere else; we'll put it in yonder,' he added, pointing vaguely toward the distance.

David screwed on the lid, while Jacob, looking grave, rose and grasped his pitchfork. Then, seeing David's bundle, he snatched it, like a too officious Newfoundland, stuck his pitchfork into it and carried it over his shoulder in triumph as he accompanied David and the box out of the thicket.

What on earth was David to do? It would have been easy to frown at Jacob, and kick him, and order him to get away; but David dared as soon have kicked the bull. Jacob was quiet as long as he was treated indulgently; but on the slightest show of anger, he became unmanageable, and was liable to fits of fury which would have made him formidable even without his pitchfork. There was no mastery to be obtained over him except by kindness or guile. David tried guile.

'Go, Jacob,' he said, when they were out of the thicket – pointing towards the house as he spoke; 'go and fetch me a spade – a spade. But give *me* the bundle, he added, trying to reach it from the fork, where it hung high above, Jacob's tall shoulder.

But Jacob showed as much alacrity in obeying as a wasp shows in leaving a sugar-basin. Near David, he felt himself in the vicinity of lozenges: he chuckled and rubbed his brother's back, brandishing the bundle higher out of reach. David, with an inward groan, changed his tactics, and walked on as fast as he could. It was not safe to linger. Jacob would get tired of following him, or, at all events, could be eluded. If they could once get to the distant highroad, a coach would overtake them, David would mount it, having previously by some ingenious means secured his bundle, and then Jacob might howl and flourish his pitchfork as much as he liked. Meanwhile he was under the fatal necessity of being very kind to this ogre, and of providing a large breakfast for him when they stopped at a roadside inn.

It was already three hours since they had started, and David was tired. Would no coach be coming up soon? he inquired. No coach for the next two hours. But there was a carrier's cart to come immediately, on its way to the next town. If he could slip out, even leaving his bundle behind, and get into the cart without Jacob! But there was a new obstacle. Jacob had recently discovered a remnant of sugar-candy in one of his brother's tail-pockets; and, since then, had cautiously kept his hold on that limb of the garment, perhaps with an expectation that there would be a further development of sugar-candy after a longer or shorter interval. Now every one who has worn a coat will understand the sensibilities that must keep a man from starting away in a hurry when there is a grasp on his coat-tail. David looked forward to being well received among strangers, but it might make a difference if he had only one tail to his coat.

He felt himself in a cold perspiration. He would walk no more: he must get into the cart and let Jacob get in with him. Presently a cheering idea occurred to him: after so large a breakfast, Jacob would be sure to go to sleep in the cart; you see at once that David meant to seize his bundle, jump out, and be free. His expectation was partly fulfilled: Jacob did go to sleep in the cart, but it was in a peculiar attitude – it was with his arms tightly fastened round his dear brother's body; and if ever David attempted to move, the grasp tightened with the force of an affectionate boa-constrictor.

'Th'innicent's fond on you,' observed the carrier, thinking that David was probably an amiable brother, and wishing to pay him a compliment.

David groaned. The ways of thieving were not ways of   19

pleasantness. Oh, why had he an idiot brother? Or why, in general, was the world so constituted that a man could not take his mother's guineas comfortably? David became grimly speculative.

Copious dinner at noon for Jacob; but little dinner, because little appetite, for David. Instead of eating, he plied Jacob with beer; for through this liberality he descried a hope. Jacob fell into a dead sleep, at last, *without* having his arms round David, who paid the reckoning, took his bundle, and walked off. In another half-hour he was on the coach on his way to Liverpool, smiling the smile of the triumphant wicked. He was rid of Jacob – he was bound for the Indies, where a gullible princess awaited him. He would never steal any more, but there would be no need; he would show himself so deserving, that people would make him presents freely. He must give up the notion of his father's legacy; but it was not likely he would ever want that trifle; and even if he did – why, it was a compensation to think that in being for ever divided from his family he was divided from Jacob, more terrible than Gorgon or Demogorgon to David's timid green eyes. Thank heaven, he should never see Jacob any more!

Chapter 2

It was nearly six years after the departure of Mr David Faux for the West Indies, that the vacant shop in the market-place at Grimworth was understood to have been let to the stranger with a sallow complexion and a buff cravat, whose first appearance had caused some excitement in the bar of the Woolpack, where he had called to wait for the coach.

Grimworth, to a discerning eye, was a good place to set up shopkeeping in. There was no competition in it at present; the Church-people had their own grocer and draper; the Dissenters had theirs; and the two or three butchers found a ready market for their joints without strict reference to religious persuasion – except that the rector's wife had given a general order for the veal sweet-breads and the mutton kidneys, while Mr Rodd, the Baptist minister, had requested that, so far as was compatible with the fair accommodation of other customers, the sheep's trotters might be reserved for him. And it was likely to be a growing place, for the trustees of Mr Zephaniah Crypt's Charity, under the stimulus of late visitation by commissioners, were beginning to apply long-accumulating funds to the rebuild-ing of the Yellow Coat School, which was henceforth to be carried forward on a greatly-extended scale, the testator having left no restrictions concerning the curriculum, but only concerning the coat.

The shopkeepers at Grimworth were by no means unanimous as to the advantages promised by this prospect of increased population and trading, being substantial men, who liked doing a quiet business in which they were sure of their customers, and could calculate their returns to a nicety. Hitherto, it had been held a point of honour by the families in Grimworth parish, to buy their sugar and their flannel at the shops where their fathers and mothers had bought before them; but, if new-comers were to bring in the system of neck-and-neck trading, and solicit feminine eyes by gown-pieces laid in fan-like folds, and surmounted by artificial flowers, giving them a factitious charm (for on what human figure would a gown sit like a fan, or what female head was like a bunch of China-asters?), or, if new grocers were to fill their windows with mountains of currants and sugar, made seductive by contrast and tickets, – what security was there for Grimworth, that a vagrant spirit in shopping, once introduced, would not in the end carry the most important families to the larger market town of Cattleton, where, business being done on a system of small profits and quick returns, the fashions were of the freshest, and goods of all kinds might be bought at an advantage?

With this view of the times predominant among the tradespeople at Grimworth, their uncertainty concerning the nature of the business which the sallow-complexioned stranger was about to set up in the vacant shop, naturally gave some additional strength to the fears of the less sanguine. If he was going to sell drapery, it was probably that a pale-faced fellow like that would deal in showy and inferior articles – printed cottons and muslins which would leave their dye in the wash-tub, jobbed linen full of knots, and flannel that would soon look like gauze. If grocery, then it was to be hoped that no mother of a family would trust the teas of an untried grocer. Such things had been known in some parishes as tradesmen going about canvassing for custom with cards in their pockets: when people came from nobody knew where, there was no knowing what they might do. It was a thousand pities that Mr Moffat, the auctioneer and broker, had died without leaving anybody to follow him in the business, and Mrs Cleve's trustee ought to have known better than to let a shop to a stranger. Even the discovery that ovens were being put up on the premises, and that the shop was, in fact, being fitted up for a confectioner and pastry-cook's business, hitherto unknown in Grimworth, did not quite suffice to turn the scale in the new-comer's favour, though the landlady at the Woolpack defended him warmly, said he seemed to be a very clever young man, and from what she could make out, came of a very good family; indeed, was most likely a good many people's betters.

It certainly made a blaze of light and colour, almost as if a rainbow had suddenly descended into the market-place, when, one fine morning, the shutters were taken down from the new shop, and the two windows displayed their decorations. On one side, there were the variegated tints of collared and marbled meats, set off by bright green leaves, the pale brown of glazed pies, rich tones of sauces and bottled fruits enclosed in their veil of glass – altogether a sight to bring tears into the eyes of a Dutch painter; and on the other, there was a predominance of the more delicate hues of pink, and white, and yellow, and buff, in the abundant lozenges, candies, sweet buscuits and icings, which to the eyes of a bilious person might easily have been blended into a faëry landscape in Turner's latest style. What a sight to dawn upon the eyes of Grimworth children! They almost forgot to go to their dinner that day, their appetites being preoccupied with imaginary sugar-plums; and I think even Punch, setting up his tabernacle in the market-place, would not have succeeded in drawing them away from those shop-windows, where they stood according to gradations of size and strength, the biggest and strongest being nearest the window, and the little ones in the outermost rows lifting wide-open eyes and mouths towards the upper tier of jars, like small birds at meal-time.

The elder inhabitants pished and pshawed a little at the folly of the new shopkeeper in venturing on such an outlay in goods that would not keep; to be sure, Christmas was coming, but what housewife in Grimworth would not think shame to furnish forth her table with articles that were not home-cooked? No, no. Mr Edward Freely, as he called himself, was deceived, if he thought Grimworth money was to flow into his pockets on such terms.

Edward Freely was the name that shone in gilt letters on a mazarine ground over the doorplace of the new shop – a generous-sounding name, that might have belonged to the open-hearted, improvident hero of an old comedy, who would have delighted in raining sugared almonds, like a 24 new manna-gift, among that small generation outside the windows. But Mr Edward Freely was a man whose impulses were kept in due subordination: he held that the desire for sweets and pastry must only be satisfied in a direct ratio with the power of paying for them. If the smallest child in Grimworth would go to him with a halfpenny in its tiny fist, he would, after ringing the halfpenny, deliver a just equivalent in 'rock'. He was not a man to cheat even the smallest child – he often said so, observing at the same time that he loved honesty, and also that he was very tenderhearted, though he didn't show his feelings as some people did.

Either in reward of such virtue, or according to some more hidden law of sequence, Mr Freely's business, in spite of prejudice, started under favourable auspices. For Mrs Chaloner, the rector's wife, was among the earliest customers at the shop, thinking it only right to encourage a new parishioner who had made a decorous appearance at church; and she found Mr Freely a most civil, obliging young man, and intelligent to a surprising degree for a confectioner; well-principled, too, for in giving her useful hints about choosing sugars he had thrown much light on the dishonesty of other tradesmen. Moreover, he had been in the West Indies, and had seen the very estate which had been her poor grandfather's property; and he said the missionaries were the only cause of the negro's discontent – an observing young man, evidently. Mrs Chaloner ordered wine-biscuits and olives, and gave Mr Freely to understand that she should find his shop a great convenience. So did the doctor's wife, and so did Mrs Gate, at the large cardingmill, who having high connections frequently visiting her, might be expected to have a large consumption of ratafias and macaroons.

The less aristocratic matrons of Grimworth seemed likely at first to justify their husbands' confidence that they would never pay a percentage of profits on drop-cakes, instead of making their own, or get up a hollow show of liberal housekeeping by purchasing slices of collared meat when a neighbour came in for supper. But it is my task to narrate the gradual corruption of Grimworth manners from their primitive simplicity – a melancholy task, if it were not cheered by the prospect of the fine peripateia or downfall by which the progress of the corruption was ultimately checked.

It was young Mrs Steene, the veterinary surgeon's wife, who first gave way to temptation. I fear she had been rather over-educated for her station in life, for she knew by heart many passages in 'Lalla Rookh', the 'Corsair', and the 'Siege of Corinth', which had given her a distaste for domestic occupations, and caused her a withering disappointment at the discovery that Mr Steene, since his marriage, had lost all interest in the 'bulbul', openly preferred discussing the nature of spavin with a coarse neighbour, and was angry if the pudding turned out watery – indeed, was simply a top-booted 'vet', who came in hungry at dinner-time; and not in the least like a nobleman turned Corsair out of pure scorn for his race, or like a renegade with a turban and crescent, unless it were in the irritability of his temper. And scorn is such a very different thing in top-boots!

This brutal man had invited a supper-party for Christmas

eve, when he would expect to see mince-pies on the table. Mrs Steene had prepared her mince-meat, and had devoted much butter, fine flour, and labour, to the making of a batch of pies in the morning; but they proved to be so very heavy when they came out of the oven, that she could only think with trembling of the moment when her husband should catch sight of them on the supper-table. He would storm at her, she was certain; and before all the company; and then she should never help crying: it was so dreadful to think she had come to that, after the bulbul and everything! Suddenly the thought darted through her mind that *this once* she might send for a dish of mince-pies from Freely's: she knew he had some. But what was to become of the eighteen heavy mince-pies? Oh, it was of no use thinking about that; it was very expensive – indeed, making mince-pies at all was a great expense, when they were not sure to turn out well: it would be much better to buy them ready-made. You paid a little more for them, but there was no risk of waste.

Such was the sophistry with which this misguided young woman – enough. Mrs Steene sent for the mince-pies, and, I am grieved to add, garbled her household accounts in order to conceal the fact from her husband. This was the second step in a downward course, all owing to a young woman's being out of harmony with her circumstances, yearning after renegades and bulbuls, and being subject to claims from a veterinary surgeon fond of mince-pies. The third step was to harden herself by telling the fact of the bought mince-pies to her intimate friend Mrs Mole, who had already guessed it, and who subsequently encouraged herself in buying a mould of jelly, instead of exerting her own skill, by the reflection that 'other people' did the same sort of thing. The infection spread; soon there was a party or clique in Grimworth on the side of 'buying at Freely's'; and many husbands, kept for some time in the dark on this point, innocently swallowed at two mouthfuls a tart on which they were paying a profit of a hundred per cent, and as innocently encouraged a fatal disingenuousness in the partners of their bosoms by praising the pastry. Others, more keen-sighted, winked at the too frequent presentation on washing-days, and at impromptu suppers, of superior spiced-beef, which flattered their palates more than the cold remnants they had formerly been contented with. Every housewife who had once 'bought at Freely's' felt a secret joy when she detected a similar perversion in her neighbour's practice, and soon only two or three old-fashioned mistresses of families held out in the protest against the growing demoralisation, saying to their neighbours who came to sup with them, 'I can't offer you Freely's beef, or Freely's cheese-cakes; everything in our house is home-made; I'm afraid you'll hardly have any appetite for our plain pastry.' The doctor, whose cook was not satisfactory, the curate, who kept no cook, and the mining agent, who was a great *bon vivant*, even began to rely on Freely for the greater part of their dinner, when they wished to give an entertainment of some brilliancy. In short, the business of manufacturing the more fanciful viands was fast passing out of the hands of maids and matrons in private families, and was becoming the work of a special commercial organ.

I am not ignorant that this sort of thing is called the inevitable course of civilisation, division of labour, and so forth, and that the maids and matrons may be said to have had their hands set free from cookery to add to the wealth of society in some other way. Only it happened at Grimworth, which, to be sure, was a low place, that the maids and matrons could do nothing with their hands at all better than cooking; not even those who had always made heavy cakes and leathery pastry. And so it came to pass, that the progress of civilisation at Grimworth was not otherwise apparent than in the impoverishment of men, the gossiping idleness of women, and the heightening prosperity of Mr Edward Freely.

The Yellow Coat School was a double source of profit to the calculating confectioner; for he opened an eating-room for the superior workmen employed on the new school, and he accommodated the pupils at the old school by giving great attention to the fancy-sugar department. When I think of sweet-tasted swans and other ingenious white shapes crunched by the small teeth of that rising generation, I am glad to remember that a certain amount of calcareous food has been held good for young creatures whose bones are not quite formed; for I have observed these delicacies to have an inorganic flavour which would have recommended them greatly to that young lady of the 'Spectator's' acquaintance who habitually made her dessert on the stems of tobacco-pipes.

As for the confectioner himself, he made his way gradually into Grimworth homes, as his commodities did, in spite of some initial repugnance. Somehow or other, his reception as a guest seemed a thing that required justifying, like the purchasing of his pastry. In the first place, he was a stranger, and therefore open to suspicion; secondly, the confectionery business was so entirely new at Grimworth, that its place in the scale of rank had not been distinctly ascertained. There was no doubt about drapers and grocers, when they came of good old Grimworth families, like Mr Luff and Mr Prettyman: they visited with the Palfreys, who farmed their own land, played many a game at whist with the doctor, and condescended a little towards the timber-merchant, who had lately taken to the coal-trade also, and had got new furniture; but whether a confectioner should be admitted to this higher level of respectability, or should be understood to find his associates among butchers and bakers, was a new question on which tradition threw no light. His being a bachelor was in his favour, and would perhaps have been enough to turn the scale, even if Mr Edward Freely's other personal pretensions had been of an entirely insignificant cast. But so far from this, it very soon appeared that he was a remarkable young man, who had been in the West Indies, and had seen many wonders by sea and land, so that he could charm the ears of Grimworth Desdemonas with stories of strange fishes, especially sharks, which he had stabbed in the nick of time by bravely plunging overboard just as the monster was turning on his side to devour the cook's mate; of terrible fevers which he had undergone in a land where the wind blows from all quarters at once; of rounds of toast cut straight from the bread-fruit trees; of toes bitten off by land-crabs; of large honours that had been offered to him as a man who knew what was what, and was therefore particularly needed in a tropical climate; and of a Creole heiress who had wept bitterly at his departure. Such conversational talents as these, we know, will overcome disadvantages of complexion; and young Towers, whose cheeks were of the finest pink, set off by a fringe of dark whisker, was quite eclipsed by the presence of the sallow Mr Freely. So exceptional a confectioner elevated his business, and might well begin to make disengaged hearts flutter a little.

Fathers and mothers were naturally more slow and cautious in their recognition of the new-comer's merits. 'He's an amusing fellow,' said Mr Prettyman, the highly respectable grocer. (Mrs Prettyman was a Miss Fothergill, and her sister had married a London mercer.) 'He's an amusing fellow; and I've no objection to his making one at the Oyster Club; but he's a bit too fond of riding the high horse. He's uncommonly knowing, I'll allow; but how came he to go to the Indies? I should like that answered. It's unnatural in a confectioner. I'm not fond of people that have been beyond seas, if they can't give a good account how they happened to go. When folks go so far off, it's because they've got little credit nearer home – that's my opinion. However, he's got some good rum; but I don't want to be hand and glove with him, for all that.'

It was this kind of dim suspicion which beclouded the view of Mr Freely's qualities in the maturer minds of Grimworth through the early months of his residence there. But when the confectioner ceased to be a novelty, the suspicions also ceased to be novel, and people got tired of hinting at them, especially as they seemed to be refuted by his advancing prosperity and importance. Mr Freely was becoming a person of influence in the parish; he was found useful as an overseer of the poor, having great firmness in enduring other people's pain, which firmness, he said, was due to his great benevolence; he always did what was good for people in the end. Mr Chaloner had even selected him as clergyman's churchwarden, for he was a very handy man, and much more of Mr Chaloner's opinion in everything about church business than the older parishioners. Mr Freely was a very regular churchman, but at the Oyster Club he was sometimes a little free in his conversation, more than hinting at a life of Sultanic self-indulgence which he had passed in the West Indies, shaking his head now and then and smiling rather bitterly, as men are wont to do when they intimate that they have become a little too wise to be instructed about a world which has long been flat and stale to them.

For some time he was quite general in his attentions to the fair sex, combining the gallantries of a lady's man with a severity of criticism on the person and manners of absent belles, which tended rather to stimulate in the feminine breast the desire to conquer the approval of so fastidious a judge. Nothing short of the very best in the department of female charms and virtues could suffice to kindle the ardour of Mr Edward Freely, who had become familiar with the most luxuriant and dazzling beauty in the West Indies. It may seem incredible that a confectioner should have ideas and conversation so much resembling those to be met with in a higher walk of life, but it must be remembered that he had not merely travelled, he had also bow-legs and a sallow, small-featured visage, so that nature herself had stamped him for a fastidious connoisseur of the fair sex.

At last, however, it seemed clear that Cupid had found a sharper arrow than usual, and that Mr Freely's heart was pierced. It was the general talk among the young people at Grimworth. But was it really love? and not rather ambition? Miss Fullilove, the timber-merchant's daughter, was quite sure that if *she* were Miss Penny Palfrey, she would be cautious; it was not a good sign when men looked so much above themselves for a wife. For it was no less a person than Miss Penelope Palfrey, second daughter of the Mr Palfrey who farmed his own land, that had attracted Mr Freely's peculiar regard, and conquered his fastidiousness; and no wonder; for the Ideal, as exhibited in the finest waxwork, was perhaps never so closely approached by the Real as in the person of the pretty Penelope. Her yellowish flaxen hair did not curl naturally, I admit, but its bright crisp ringlets were such smooth, perfect miniature tubes, that you would have longed to pass your little finger through them, and feel their soft elasticity. She wore them in a crop, for in those days, when society was in a healthier state, young ladies wore crops long after they were twenty, and Penelope was not yet nineteen. Like the waxen ideal, she had round blue eyes, and round nostrils in her little nose, and teeth such as the ideal would be seen to have, if it ever showed them. Altogether, she was a small, round thing, as neat as a pink and white double daisy, and as guileless; for I hope it does not argue guile in a pretty damsel of nineteen, to think that she should like to have a beau and be 'engaged', when her elder sister had already been in that position a year and a half. To be sure, there was young Towers always coming to the house; but Penny felt convinced he only came to see her brother, for he never had anything to say to her, and never offered her his arm, and was as awkward and silent as possible.

It is not unlikely that Mr Freely had early been smitten by Penny's charms, as brought under his observation at church, but he had to make his way in society a little before he could come into nearer contact with them; and even after he was well received in Grimworth families, it was a long while before he could converse with Penny otherwise than in an incidental meeting at Mr Luff's. It was not so easy to get invited to Long Meadows, the residence of the Palfreys; for though Mr Palfrey had been losing money of late years, not being able quite to recover his feet after the terrible murrain which forced him to borrow, his family were far from considering themselves on the same level even as the old-established tradespeople with whom they visited. The greatest people, even kings and queens, must visit with somebody, and the equals of the great are scarce. They were especially scarce at Grimworth, which, as I have before observed, was a low parish, mentioned with the most scornful brevity in gazetteers. Even the great people there were far behind those of their own standing in other parts of this realm. Mr Palfrey's farmyard doors had the paint all worn off them, and the front garden walks had long been merged in a general weediness. Still, his father had been called Squire Palfrey, and had been respected by the last Grimworth generation as a man who could afford to drink too much in his own house.

Pretty Penny was not blind to the fact that Mr Freely admired her, and she felt sure that it was he who had sent her a beautiful valentine; but her sister seemed to think so lightly of him (all young ladies think lightly of the gentlemen to whom they are not engaged), that Penny never dared mention him, and trembled and blushed whenever they met him, thinking of the valentine, which was very strong in its expressions, and which she felt guilty of knowing by heart. A man who had been to the Indies, and knew the sea so well, seemed to her a sort of public character, almost like Robinson Crusoe or Captain Cook; and Penny had always wished her husband to be a remarkable personage, likely to be put in Mangnall's Questions, with which register of the immortals she had become acquainted during her one a year at a boarding-school. Only it seemed strange that a remarkable man should be a confectioner and pastry-cook, and this anomaly quite disturbed Penny's dreams. Her brothers, she knew, laughed at men who couldn't sit on horseback well, and called them tailors; but her brothers were very rough, and were quite without that power of anecdote which made Mr Freely such a delightful companion. He was a very good man, she thought, for she had heard him say at Mr Luff's, one day, that he always wished to do his duty in whatever state of life he might be placed; and he knew a great deal of poetry, for one day he had repeated a verse of a song. She wondered if he had made the words of the valentine! – it ended in this way:

> Without thee, it is pain to live,
> But with thee, it were sweet to die.

Poor Mr Freely! her father would very likely object – she

felt sure he would, for he always called Mr Freely 'that sugar-plum fellow'. Oh, it was very cruel, when true love was crossed in that way, and all because Mr Freely was a confectioner: well, Penny would be true to him, for all that, and since his being a confectioner gave her an opportunity of showing her faithfulness, she was glad of it. Edward Freely was a pretty name, much better than John Towers. Young Towers had offered her a rose out of his button-hole the other day, blushing very much; but she refused it, and thought with delight how much Mr Freely would be comforted if he knew her firmness of mind.

Poor little Penny! the days were so very long among the daisies on a grazing farm, and thought is so active – how was it possible that the inward drama should not get the start of the outward? I have known young ladies, much better educated, and with an outward world diversified by instructive lectures, to say nothing of literature and highly-developed fancy-work, who have spun a cocoon of visionary joys and sorrows for themselves, just as Penny did. Her elder sister Letitia, who had a prouder style of beauty, and a more worldly ambition, was engaged to a wool-factor, who came all the way from Cattelton to see her; and everybody knows that a wool-factor takes a very high rank, sometimes driving a double-bodied gig. Letty's notions got higher every day, and Penny never dared to speak of her cherished griefs to her lofty sister – never dared to propose that they should call at Mr Freely's to buy liquorice, though she had prepared for such an incident by mentioning a slight sore throat. So she had to pass the shop on the other side of the market-place, and reflect, with a suppressed sigh, that behind those pink and white jars somebody was thinking of her tenderly, unconscious of the small space that divided her from him.

And it was quite true that, when business permitted, Mr Freely thought a great deal of Penny. He thought her prettiness comparable to the loveliest things in confectionery; he judged her to be of submissive temper – likely to wait upon him as well as if she had been a negress, and to be silently terrified when his liver made him irritable; and he considered the Palfrey family quite the best in the parish, possessing marriageable daughters. On the whole, he thought her worthy to become Mrs Edward Freely, and all the more so, because it would probably require some ingenuity to win her. Mr Palfrey was capable of horse-whipping a too rash pretender to his daughter's hand; and, moreover, he had three tall sons: it was clear that a suitor would be at a disadvantage with such a family, unless travel and natural acumen had given him a countervailing power of contrivance. And the first idea that occurred to him in the matter was, that Mr Palfrey would object less if he knew that the Freelys were a much higher family than his own. It had been foolish modesty in him hitherto to conceal the fact that a branch of the Freelys held a manor in Yorkshire, and to shut up the portrait of his great uncle the admiral, instead of hanging it up where a family portrait should be hung – over the mantelpiece in the parlour. Admiral Freely, K.C.B., once placed in this conspicuous position, was seen to have had one arm only, and one eye, – in these points resembling the heroic Nelson, while a certain pallid insignificance of feature confirmed the relationship between himself and his grand-nephew.

Next, Mr Freely was seized with an irrepressible ambition to possess Mrs Palfrey's receipt for brawn, hers being pronounced on all hands to be superior to his own – as he informed her in a very flattering letter carried by his errand-boy. Now Mrs Palfrey, like other geniuses, wrought by instinct rather than by rule, and possessed no receipts, – indeed, despised all people who used them, observing that people who pickled by book, must pickle by weights and measures, and such nonsense; as for herself, her weights and measures were the tip of her finger and the tip of her tongue, and if you went nearer, why, of course, for dry goods like flour and spice, you went by handfuls and pinches, and for wet, there was a middle-sized jug – quite the best thing whether for much or little, because you might know how much a teacupful was if you'd got any use of your senses, and you might be sure it would take five middle-sized jugs to make a gallon. Knowledge of this kind is like Titian's colouring, difficult to communicate; and as Mrs Palfrey, once remarkably handsome, had now become rather stout and asthmatical, and scarcely ever left home, her oral teaching could hardly be given anywhere except at Long Meadows. Even a matron is not insusceptible to flattery, and the prospect of a visitor whose great object would be to listen to her conversation, was not without its charms to Mrs Palfrey. Since there was no receipt to be sent in reply to Mr Freely's humble request, she called on her more docile daughter, Penny, to write a note, telling him that her mother would be glad to see him and talk with him on brawn, any day that he could call at Long Meadows.

Penny obeyed with a trembling hand, thinking how wonderfully things came about in this world.

In this way, Mr Freely got himself introduced into the home of the Palfreys, and notwithstanding a tendency in the male part of the family to jeer at him a little as 'peaky' and bow-legged, he presently established his position as an accepted and frequent guest. Young Towers looked at him with increasing disgust when they met at the house on a Sunday, and secretly longed to try his ferret upon him, as a piece of vermin which that valuable animal would be likely to tackle with unhesitating vigour. But – so blind sometimes are parents – neither Mr nor Mrs Palfrey suspected that Penny would have anything to say to a tradesman of questionable rank whose youthful bloom was much withered. Young Towers, they thought, had an eye to her, and *that* was likely enough to be a match some day; but Penny was a child at present. And all the while Penny was imagining the circumstances under which Mr Freely would make her an offer: perhaps down by the row of damson-trees, when they were in the garden before tea; perhaps by letter – in which case, how would be letter begin? 'Dearest Penelope?' or 'My dear Miss Penelope?' or straight off, without dear anything, as seemed the most natural when people were embarrassed? But, however he might make the offer, she would not accept it without her father's consent: she would always be true to Mr Freely, but she would not disobey her father. For Penny was a good girl, though some of her female friends were afterwards of opinion that it spoke ill for her not to have felt an instinctive repugnance to Mr Freely.

But he was cautious, and wished to be quite sure of the ground he trod on. His views in marriage were not entirely sentimental, but were as duly mingled with considerations of what would be advantageous to a man in his position, as if he had had a very large amount of money spent on his education. He was not a man to fall in love in the wrong place; and so, he applied himself quite as much to conciliate the favour of the parents, as to secure the attachment of Penny. Mrs Palfrey had not been inaccessible to flattery, and her husband, being also of mortal mould, would not, it might be hoped, be proof against rum – that very fine Jamaica rum of which Mr Freely expected always to have a supply sent him from Jamaica. It was not easy to get Mr Palfrey into the parlour behind the shop, where a mild back-street light fell on the features of the heroic admiral; but by getting hold of him rather late one evening as he was about to return home from Grimworth, the aspiring lover succeeded in persuading him to sup on some collared beef which, after Mrs Palfrey's brawn, he would find the very best of cold eating.

From that hour Mr Freely felt sure of success: being in privacy with an estimable man old enough to be his father, and being rather lonely in the world, it was natural he should unbosom himself a little on subjects which he could not speak of in a mixed circle – especially concerning his expectations from his uncle in Jamaica, who had no children, and loved his nephew Edward better than any one else in the world, though he had been so hurt at his leaving Jamaica, that he had threatened to cut him off with a shilling. However, he had since written to state his full forgiveness, and though he was an eccentric old gentleman and could not bear to give away money during his life, Mr Edward Freely could show Mr Palfrey the letter which declared, plainly enough, who would be the affectionate uncle's heir. Mr Palfrey actually saw the letter, and could not help admiring the spirit of the nephew who declared that such brilliant hopes as these made no difference to his conduct; he should work at his humble business and make his modest fortune at it all the same. If the Jamaica estate was to come to him – well and good. It was nothing very surprising for one of the Freely family to have an estate left him, considering the lands that family had possessed in time gone by, – nay, still possessed in the Northumberland branch. Would not Mr Palfrey take another glass of rum? and also look at the last year's balance of the accounts? Mr Freely was a man who cared to possess personal virtues, and did not pique himself on his family, though some men would.

We know how easily the great Leviathan may be led, when once there is a hook in his nose or a bridle in his jaw. Mr Palfrey was a large man, but, like Leviathan's, his bulk went against him when once he had taken a turning. He was not a mercurial man, who easily changed his point of view. Enough. Before two months were over, he had given his consent to Mr Freely's marriage with his daughter Penny, and having hit on a formula by which he could justify it, fenced off all doubts and objections, his own included. The formula was this: 'I'm not a man to put my head up an entry before I know where it leads.'

Little Penny was very proud and fluttering, but hardly so

happy as she expected to be in an engagement. She wondered if young Towers cared much about it, for he had not been to the house lately, and her sister and brothers were rather inclined to sneer than to sympathise. Grimworth rang with the news. All men extolled Mr Freely's good fortune; while the women, with the tender solicitude characteristic of the sex, wished the marriage might turn out well.

While affairs were at this triumphant juncture, Mr Freely one morning observed that a stone-carver who had been breakfasting in the eating-room had left a newspaper behind. It was the 'X – shire Gazette', and X – shire being a country not unknown to Mr Freely, he felt some curiosity to glance over it, and especially over the advertisements. A slight flush came over his face as he read. It was produced by the following announcement: 'If David Faux, son of Jonathan Faux, late of Gilsbrook, will apply at the office of Mr Strutt, attorney, of Rodham, he will hear of something to his advantage.'

'Father's dead!' exclaimed Mr Freely, involuntarily. 'Can he have left me a legacy?'

CHAPTER 3

Perhaps it was a result quite different from your expectations, that Mr David Faux should have returned from the West Indies only a few years after his arrival there, and have set up in his old business, like any plain man who had never travelled. But these cases do occur in life. Since, as we know, men change their skies and see new constellations without changing their souls, it will follow sometimes that they don't change their business under those novel circumstances.

Certainly, this result was contrary to David's own expectations. He had looked forward, you are aware, to a brilliant career among 'the blacks'; but, either because they had already seen too many white men, or for some other reason, they did not at once recognise him as a superior order of human being; besides, there were no princesses among them. Nobody in Jamaica was anxious to maintain David for the mere pleasure of his society; and those hidden merits of a man which are so well known to himself were as little recognised there as they notoriously are in the effete society of the Old World. So that in the dark hints that David threw out at the Oyster Club about that life of Sultanic self-indulgence spent by him in the luxurious Indies, I really think he was doing himself a wrong; I believe he worked for his bread, and, in fact, took to cooking again, as after all, the only department in which he could offer skilled labour. He had formed several ingenious plans by which he meant to circumvent people of large fortune and small faculty; but then he never met with exactly the right people under exactly the right circumstances. David's devices for getting rich without work had apparently no direct relation with the world outside him, as his confectionery receipts had. It is possible to pass a great many bad halfpennies and bad half-crowns, but I believe there has no instance been known of passing a halfpenny or a half-crown as a sovereign. A sharper can drive a brisk trade in this world: it is undeniable that there may be a fine career for him, if he will dare consequences; but David was too timid to be a sharper, or venture in any way among the mantraps of the law. He dared rob nobody but his mother. And so he had to fall back on the genuine value there was in him – to be content to pass as a good halfpenny, or, to speak more accurately, as a good confectioner. For in spite of some additional reading and observation, there was nothing else he could make so much money by; nay, he found in himself even a capability of cookery; while, in other branches of human labour, he began to see that it was not possible for him to shine. Fate was too strong for him; he had thought to master her inclination and had fled over the seas to that end; but she caught him, tied an apron round him, and snatching him from all other devices, made him devise cakes and patties in a kitchen at Kingstown. He was getting submissive to her, since she paid him with tolerable gains; but fevers and prickly heat, and other evils incidental to cooks in ardent climates, made him long for his native land; so he took ship once more, carrying his six years' savings, and seeing distinctly, this time, what were Fate's intentions as to his career. If you question me closely as to whether all the money with which he set up at Grimworth consisted of pure and simple earnings, I am obliged to confess that he got a sum or two for charitably abstaining from mentioning some other people's misdemeanours. Altogether, since no prospects were attached to his family name, and since a new christening seemed a suitable commencement of a new life, Mr David Faux thought it as well to call himself Mr Edward Freely.

But lo! now, in opposition to all calculable probability, some benefit appeared to be attached to the name of David Faux. Should he neglect it, as beneath the attention of prosperous tradesman? It might bring him into contact with his family again, and he felt no yearnings in that direction: moreover, he had small belief that the 'something to his advantage' could be anything considerable. On the other hand, even a small gain is pleasant, and the promise of it in this instance was so surprising, that David felt his curiosity awakened. The scale dipped at last on the side of writing to the lawyer, and, to be brief, the correspondence ended in an appointment for a meeting between David and his eldest brother at Mr Stutt's, the vague 'something' having been defined as a legacy from his father of eighty-two pounds three shillings.

David, you know, had expected to be disinherited; and so he would have been, if he had not, like some other indifferent sons, come of excellent parents, whose conscience made them scrupulous where much more highly-instructed people often feel themselves warranted in following the bent of their indignation. Good Mrs Faux could never forget that she had brought this ill-conditioned son into the world when he was in that entirely helpless state which excluded the smallest choice on his part; and, somehow or other, she felt that his going wrong would be his father's and mother's fault, if they failed in one tittle of their parental duty. Her notion of parental duty was not of a high and subtle kind, but it included giving him his due share of the family property; for when a man had got a little honest money of his own, was he so likely to steal? To cut the dilinquent son off with a shilling, was like delivering him over to his evil propensities. No; let the sum of twenty guineas which he had stolen be deducted from his share, and then let the sum of three guineas be put back from it, seeing that his mother had always considered three of the twenty guineas as his; and, though he had run away, and was, perhaps, gone across the sea, let the money be left to him all the same, and be kept in reserve for his possible return. Mr Faux agreed to his wife's views, and made a codicil to his will accordingly, in time to die with a clear conscience. But for some time his family thought it likely that David would never reappear; and the eldest son, who had the charge of Jacob on his hands, often thought it a little hard that David might perhaps be dead, and yet, for want of certitude on that point, his legacy could not fall to his legal heir. But in this state of things the opposite certitude – namely, that David was still alive and in England – seemed to be brought by the testimony of a neighbour, who, having been on a journey, to Cattleton, was pretty sure he had seen David in a gig, with a stout man driving by his side. He could 'swear it was David', though he could 'give no account why, for he had no marks on him; but no more had a white dog, and that didn't hinder folks from knowing a white dog'. It was this incident which had led to the advertisement.

The legacy was paid, of course, after a few preliminary disclosures as to Mr David's actual position. He begged to send his love to his mother, and to say that he hoped to pay her a dutiful visit by-and-by; but, at present, his business and near prospect of marriage made it difficult for him to leave home. His brother replied with much frankness.

'My mother may do as she likes about having you to see her, but, for my part, I don't want to catch sight of you on the premises again. When folks have taken a new name, they'd better keep to their new 'quinetance.'

David pocketed the insult along with the eighty-two pounds three, and travelled home again in some triumph at the ease of a transaction which had enriched him to this extent. He had no intention of offending his brother by further claims on his fraternal recognition, and relapsed with full contentment into the character of Mr Edward Freely, the orphan, scion of a great but reduced family, with an eccentric uncle in West Indies. (I have already hinted that he had some acquaintance with imaginative literature; and being of a practical turn, he had, you perceive, applied even this form of knowledge to practical purposes.)

It was little more than a week after the return from his fruitful journey, that the day of his marriage with Penny 47 having been fixed, it was agreed that Mrs Palfrey should overcome her reluctance to move from home, and that she and her husband should bring their two daughters to inspect little Penny's future abode and decide on the new arrangements to be made for the reception of the bride. Mr Freely meant her to have a house so pretty and comfortable that she need not envy even a wool-factor's wife. Of course, the upper room over the shop was to be the best sitting-room; but also the parlour behind the shop was to be made a suitable bower for the lovely Penny, who would naturally wish to be near her husband, though Mr Freely declared his resolution never to allow *his* wife to wait in the shop. The decisions about the parlour furniture were left till last, because the party was to take tea there; and, about five o'clock, they were all seated there with the best muffins and buttered buns before them, little Penny blushing and smiling, with her 'crop' in the best order, and a blue frock showing her little white shoulders, while her opinion was being always asked and never given. She secretly wished to have a particular sort of chimney ornaments, but she could not have brought herself to mention it. Seated by the side of her yellow and rather withered lover, who, though he had not reached his thirtieth year, had already crow's-feet about his eyes, she was quite tremulous at the greatness of her lot in being married to a man who had travelled so much – and before her sister Letty! The handsome Letitia looked rather proud and contemptuous, thought her future brother-in-law an odious person, and was vexed with her father and mother for letting Penny marry him. Dear little Penny! She certainly did look like a fresh white-heart cherry going to be bitten off the stem by that lipless mouth. Would no deliverer come to make a slip between that cherry and that mouth without a lip?

'Quite a family likeness between the admiral and you, Mr Freely,' observed Mrs Palfrey, who was looking at the family portrait for the first time. 'It's wonderful! and only a grand-uncle. Do you feature the rest of your family, as you know of?'

'I can't say,' said Mr Freely, with a sigh. 'My family have mostly thought themselves too high to take any notice of me.'

At this moment an extraordinary disturbance was heard in the shop, as of a heavy animal stamping about and making angry noises, and then of a glass vessel falling in shivers, while the voice of the apprentice was heard calling 'Master' in great alarm.

Mr Freely rose in anxious astonishment, and hastened into the shop, followed by the four Palfreys, who made a group at the parlour-door, transfixed with wonder at seeing a large man in a smock-frock, with a pitchfork in his hand, rush up to Mr Freely and hug him, crying out, – 'Zavy, Zavy, b'other Zavy!'

It was Jacob, and for some moments David lost all presence of mind. He felt arrested for having stolen his mother's guineas. He turned cold, and trembled in his brother's grasp.

'Why, how's this?' said Mr Palfrey, advancing from the door. 'Who is he?'

Jacob supplied the answer by saying over and over again, –

'I'se Zacob, b'other Zacob. Come 'o zee Zavy' – till hunger prompted him to relax his grasp, and to seize a large raised pie, which he lifted to his mouth.

By this time David's power of device had begun to return, but it was a very hard task for his prudence to master his rage and hatred towards poor Jacob.

'I don't know who he is; he must be drunk,' he said, in a low tone to Mr Palfrey. 'But he's dangerous with that pitchfork. He'll never let it go.' Then checking himself on the point of betraying too great an intimacy with Jacob's habits, he added, '*You* watch him, while I run for the constable.' And he hurried out of the shop.

'Why, where do you come from, my man?' said Mr Palfrey speaking to Jacob in a conciliatory tone. Jacob was eating his pie by large mouthfuls, and looking round at the other good things in the shop, while he embraced his pitchfork with his left arm and laid his left hand on some Bath buns. He was in the rare position of a person who recovers a long absent friend and finds him richer than ever in the characteristics that won his heart.

'I's Zacob – b'other Zacob – 't home. I love Zavy – b'other Zavy,' he said, as soon as Mr Palfrey had drawn his attention. 'Zavy come back from z' Indies – got mother's zinnies. Where's Zavy?' he added, looking round and then turning to the others with a questioning air, puzzled by David's disappearance.

'It's very odd,' observed Mr Palfrey to his wife and daughters. 'He seems to say Freely's his brother come back from th' Indies.'

50 'What a pleasant relation for us!' said Letitia, sarcasti-

cally. 'I think he's a good deal like Mr Freely. He's got just the same sort of nose, and his eyes are the same colour.'

Poor Penny was ready to cry.

But now Mr Freely re-entered the shop without the constable. During his walk of a few yards he had had time and calmness enough to widen his view of consequences, and saw that to get Jacob taken to the workhouse or to the lock-up house as an offensive stranger, might have awkward effects if his family took the trouble of inquiring after him. He must resign himself to more patient measures.

'On second thoughts,' he said, beckoning to Mr Palfrey and whispering to him while Jacob's back was turned, 'he's a poor half-witted fellow. Perhaps his friends will come after him. I don't mind giving him something to eat, and letting him lie down for the night. He's got it into his head that he knows me – they do get these fancies, idiots do. He'll perhaps go away again in an hour or two, and make no more ado. I'm a kind-hearted man *myself* – I shouldn't like to have the poor fellow ill-used.'

'Why, he'll eat a sovereign's worth in no time,' said Mr Palfrey, thinking Mr Freely a little too magnificent in his generosity.

'Eh, Zavy, come back?' exclaimed Jacob, giving his dear brother another hug, which crushed Mr Freely's features inconveniently against the stake of the pitchfork.

'Ay, ay,' said Mr Freely, smiling, with every capability of murder in his mind, except the courage to commit it. He wished the Bath buns might by chance have arsenic in them.

'Mother's zinnies?' said Jacob, pointing to a glass jar of yellow lozenges that stood in the window. 'Zive 'em me.'

David dared not do otherwise than reach down the glass jar and give Jacob a handful. He received them in his smock-frock, which he held out for more.

'They'll keep him quiet a bit, at any rate,' thought David, and emptied the jar. Jacob grinned and mowed with delight.

'You're very good to this stranger, Mr Freely,' said Letitia; and then spitefully, as David joined the party at the parlour-door, 'I think you could hardly treat him better, if he was really your brother.'

'I've always thought it a duty to be good to idiots,' said Mr Freely, striving after the most moral view of the subject. 'We might have been idiots ourselves – everybody might have been born idiots, instead of having their right senses.'

'I don't know where there'd ha' been victual for us all then,' observed Mrs Palfrey, regarding the matter in a housewifely light.

'But let us sit down again and finish our tea,' said Mr Freely. 'Let us leave the poor creature to himself.'

They walked into the parlour again; but Jacob, not apparently appreciating the kindness of leaving him to himself, immediately followed his brother, and seated himself, pitchfork grounded, at the table.

'Well,' said Mrs Letitia, rising, 'I don't know whether *you* mean to stay, mother; but I shall go home.'

'Oh, me too,' said Penny, frightened to death at Jacob, who had begun to nod and grin at her.

'Well, I think we *had* better be going, Mr Palfrey,' said the mother, rising more slowly.

Mr Freely, whose complexion had become decidedly

yellower during the last half-hour, did not resist this proposition. He hoped they should meet again 'under happier circumstances'.

'It's my belief the man is his brother,' said Letitia, when they were all on their way home.

'Letty, it's very ill-natured of you,' said Penny, beginning to cry.

'Nonsense!' said Mr Palfrey. 'Freely's got no brother – he's said so many and many a time; he's an orphan; he's got nothing but uncles – leastwise, one. What's it matter what an idiot says? What call had Freely to tell lies?'

Letitia tossed her head and was silent.

Mr Freely, left alone with his affectionate brother Jacob, brooded over the possibility of luring him out of the town early the next morning, and getting him conveyed to Gilsbrook without further betrayals. But the thing was difficult. He saw clearly that if he took Jacob away himself, his absence, conjoined with the disappearance of the stranger, would either cause the conviction that he was really a relative, or would oblige him to the dangerous course of inventing a story to account for his disappearance, and his own absence at the same time. David groaned. It would, perhaps, have been a longer-headed device, if he had never told any of those clever fibs about his uncles, grand and otherwise; for the Palfreys were simple people, and shared the popular prejudice against lying. Even if he could get Jacob away this time, what security was there that he would not come again, having once found the way? O guineas! O lozenges! what enviable people those were who had never robbed their mothers, and had never told fibs!

David spent a sleepless night, while Jacob was snoring close by. Was this the upshot of travelling to the Indies, and acquiring experience combined with anecdote?

He rose at break of day, as he had once before done when he was in fear of Jacob, and took all gentle means to rouse this fatal brother from his deep sleep; he dared not be loud, because his apprentice was in the house, and would report everything. But Jacob was not to be roused. He fought out with his fist at the unknown cause of disturbance, turned over, and snored again. He must be left to wake as he would. David, with a cold perspiration on his brow, confessed to himself that Jacob could not be got away that day.

Mr Palfrey came over to Grimworth before noon, with a natural curiosity to see how his future son-in-law got on with the stranger to whom he was so benevolently inclined. He found a crowd round the shop. All Grimworth by this time had heard how Freely had been fastened on by an idiot, who called him 'Brother Zavy'; and the younger population seemed to find the singular stranger an unwearying source of fascination, while the householders dropped in one by one to inquire into the incident.

'Why don't you send him to the workhouse?' said Mr Prettyman. 'You'll have a row with him and the children presently, and he'll eat you up. The workhouse is the proper place for him; let his kin claim him, if he's got any.'

'Those may be *your* feelings, Mr Prettyman,' said David, his mind quite enfeebled by the torture of his position.

'What! *is* he your brother, then?' said Mr Prettyman, looking at his neighbour Freely rather sharply.

'All men are our brothers, and idiots particular so,' said Mr Freely, who, like many other travelled men, was not master of the English language.

'Come, come, if he's your brother, tell the truth, man,' said Mr Prettyman, with growing suspicion. 'Don't be ashamed of your own flesh and blood.'

Mr Palfrey was present, and also had his eye on Freely. It is difficult for a man to believe in the advantage of a truth which will disclose him to have been a liar. In this critical moment, David shrank from this immediate disgrace in the eyes of his future father-in-law.

'Mr Prettyman,' he said, 'I take your observations as an insult. I've no reason to be otherwise than proud of my own flesh and blood. If this poor man was my brother more than all men are, I should say so.'

A tall figure darkened the door, and David, lifting his eyes in that direction, saw his eldest brother, Jonathan, on the doorsill.

'I'll stay wi' Zavy,' shouted Jacob, as he, too, caught sight of his eldest brother; and, running behind the counter, he clutched David hard.

'What, he *is* here?' said Jonathan Faux, coming forward. 'My mother would have no nay, as he'd been away so long, but I must see after him. And it struck me he was very like come after you, because we'd been talking of you o' late, and where you lived.'

David saw there was no escape; he smiled a ghastly smile.

'What! is this a relation of yours, sir?' said Mr Palfrey to Jonathan.

'Ay, it's my innicent of a brother, sure enough,' said

55

honest Jonathan. 'A fine trouble and cost he is to us, in th' eating and other things, but we must bear what's laid on us.'

'And your name's Freely, is it?' said Mr Prettyman.

'Nay, nay, my name's Faux, I know nothing o' Freelys,' said Jonathan, curtly. 'Come,' he added, turning to David, 'I must take some news to mother about Jacob. Shall I take him with me, or will you undertake to send him back?'

'Take him, if you can make him loose his hold of me,' said David, feebly.

'Is this gentleman here in the confectionery line your brother, then, sir?' said Mr Prettyman, feeling that it was an occasion on which formal language must be used.

'*I* don't want to own him,' said Jonathan, unable to resist a movement of indignation that had never been allowed to satisfy itself. 'He run away from home with good reasons in his pocket years ago: he didn't want to be owned again, I reckon.'

Mr Palfrey left the shop; he felt his own pride too severely wounded by the sense that he had let himself be fooled, to feel curiosity for further details. The most pressing business was to go home and tell his daughter that Freely was a poor sneak, probably a rascal, and that her engagement was broken off.

Mr Prettyman stayed, with some internal self-gratulation that *he* had never given in to Freely, and that Mr Chaloner would see now what sort of fellow it was that he had put over the heads of older parishioners. He considered it due from him (Mr Prettyman) that, for the interests of the parish, he should know all that was to be known about this 'interloper'. Grimworth would have people coming from

Botany Bay to settle in it, if things went on in this way.

It soon appeared that Jacob could not be made to quit his dear brother David except by force. He understood, with a clearness equal to that of the most intelligent mind, that Jonathan would take him back to skimmed milk, apple-dumpling, broad-beans, and pork. And he had found a paradise in his brother's shop. It was a difficult matter to use force with Jacob, for he wore heavily nailed boots; and if his pitchfork had been mastered, he would have resorted without hesitation to kicks. Nothing short of using guile to bind him hand and foot would have made all parties safe.

'Let him stay,' said David, with desperate resignation, frightened above all things at the idea of further disturbances in his shop, which would make his exposure all the more conspicuous. '*You* go away again, and tomorrow I can, perhaps, get him to go to Gilsbrook with me. He'll follow me fast enough, I daresay,' he added, with a half-groan.

'Very well,' said Jonathan, gruffly. 'I don't see why *you* shouldn't have some trouble and expense with him as well as the rest of us. But mind you bring him back safe and soon, else mother'll never rest.'

On this arrangement being concluded, Mr Prettyman begged Mr Jonathan Faux to go and take a snack with him, an invitation which was quite acceptable; and as honest Jonathan had nothing to be ashamed of, it is probable that he was very frank in his communications to the civil draper, who, pursuing the benefit of the parish, hastened to make all the information he could gather about Freely common parochial property. You may imagine that the meeting of the Club at the Woolpack that evening was unusually lively.

Every member was anxious to prove that he had never liked Freely, as he called himself. Faux was his name, was it? Fox would have been more suitable. The majority expressed a desire to see him hooted out of the town.

Mr Freely did not venture over his door-sill that day, for he knew Jacob would keep at his side, and there was every probability that they would have a train of juvenile followers. He sent to engage the Woolpack gig for an early hour the next morning; but this order was not kept religiously a secret by the landlord. Mr Freely was informed that he could not have the gig till seven; and the Grimworth people were early risers. Perhaps they were more alert than usual on this particular morning; for when Jacob, with a bag of sweets in his hand, was induced to mount the gig with his brother David, the inhabitants of the market-place were looking out of their doors and windows, and at the turning of the street there was even a muster of apprentices and schoolboys, who shouted as they passed in what Jacob took to be a very merry and friendly way, nodding and grinning in return. 'Huzzay, David Faux! how's your uncle?' was their morning's greeting. Like other pointed things, it was not altogether impromptu.

Even this public derision was not so crushing to David as the horrible thought that though he might succeed now in getting Jacob home again there would never be any security against his coming back, like a wasp to the honey-pot. As long as David lived at Grimworth, Jacob's return would be hanging over him. But could he go on living at Grimworth – an object of ridicule, discarded by the Palfreys, after having revelled in the consciousness that he was an envied and prosperous confectioner? David liked to be envied; he minded less about being loved.

His doubts on this point were soon settled. The mind of Grimworth became obstinately set against him and his viands, and the new school being finished, the eating-room was closed. If there had been no other reason, sympathy with the Palfreys, that respectable family who had lived in the parish time out of mind, would have determined all well-to-do people to decline Freely's goods. Besides, he had absconded with his mother's guineas: who knew what else he had done, in Jamaica or elsewhere, before he came to Grimworth, worming himself into families under false pretences? Females shuddered. Dreadful suspicions gathered round him: his green eyes, his bow-legs, had a criminal aspect. The rector disliked the sight of a man who had imposed upon him; and all boys who could not afford to purchase, hooted 'David Faux' as they passed his shop. Certainly no man now would pay anything for the 'goodwill' of Mr Freely's business, and he would be obliged to quit it without a peculium so desirable towards defraying the expense of moving.

In a few months the shop in the market-place was again to let, and Mr David Faux, *alias* Mr Edward Freely, had gone – nobody at Grimworth knew whither. In this way the demoralisation of Grimworth women was checked. Young Mrs Steene renewed her efforts to make light mince-pies, and having at last made a batch so excellent that Mr Steene looked at her with complacency as he ate them, and said they were the best he had ever eaten in his life, she thought less of bulbuls and renegades ever after. The secrets of the finer cookery were revived in the breasts of matronly housewives, and daughters were again anxious to be initiated in them.

You will further, I hope, be glad to hear, that some purchases of drapery made by pretty Penny, in preparation for her marriage with Mr Freely, came in quite as well for her wedding with young Towers as if they had been made expressly for the latter occasion. For Penny's complexion had not altered, and blue always became it best.

Here ends the story of Mr David Faux, confectioner, and his brother Jacob. And we see in it, I think, an admirable instance of the unexpected forms in which the great Nemesis hides herself.

A Note on George Eliot

George Eliot was born Mary Anne (later Mary Ann, then Marian) Evans, on 22 November 1819 at Arbury Farm in Warwickshire. When she was five months old the family moved to a farmhouse at Griff, which was her home till she was twenty-one. Her rural upbringing had a profound influence on her imagination. She attended schools at Attleborough and Nuneaton before boarding at the Misses Franklin's school in Coventry, where she studied literature in several languages, excelled in English composition and developed her musical talents.

She left school in 1835, and, after her mother's death, became her father's housekeeper. In 1841 father and daughter moved to Coventry, where Marian was introduced to Charles Bray and his wife Cara. The influence of them and their circle precipitated her move away from dogmatic belief, opening her mind to many new influences. At this time she began her translation of Strauss's *Life of Jesus* (1846): a critical account of the historical veracity of the New Testament. After her father's death in 1849 Marian Evans spent some months in Switzerland, before beginning her life in London as editor of, and contributor to, John Chapman's *Westmintser Review*. In 1852 she met G. H. Lewes, with whom she was to live (circumstances made it impossible for them to marry) until his death in 1878. With his encouragement, and using the pen-name of George Eliot to conceal her female identity, she published *Scenes of Clerical Life* and *Adam Bede*, which at once became a triumphant success. *The Lifted Veil*, *The Mill on the Floss*, *Brother Jacob*, *Silas Marner*, *Romola*, *Felix Holt*, *Middlemarch* and *Daniel Deronda* followed over the years, consolidating her reputation and her fame, as well as vanquishing the hostility which her relationship with G. H. Lewes had attracted. Her last work, *The Impressions of Theophrastus Such* was published in 1879; in the following year she married her friend of many years, J. W. Cross, but died a few months later. She is buried close to Lewes in Highgate Cemetery.